FOR DANE ANDERS AND RAINER LANE, LIGHTS OF OUR LIVES. —S.B. AND B.R.

FOR MOM —J.C.

STERLING CHILDREN'S BOOKS
New York

STERLING CHILDREN'S BOOKS
New York

An Imprint of Sterling Publishing Co., Inc.
1166 Avenue of the Americas
New York, NY 10036

Text © 2018 Shira Boss
Illustrations © 2018 Jamey Christoph
Epilogue photo © Laura Yost

STERLING CHILDREN'S BOOKS and the distinctive Sterling Children's Books logo
are registered trademarks of Sterling Publishing Co., Inc.

ISBN 978-1-4549-2071-7

Library of Congress Cataloging-in-Publication Data

Names: Boss, Shira, author. | Christoph, Jamey, illustrator.
Title: Up in the leaves : the true story of the Central Park treehouses / by
Shira Boss ; illustrated by Jamey Christoph.
Description: New York : Sterling Children's Books, [2018] | Summary: Bob does
not like the noisy, crowded streets and school hallways of his New York
City home, so he decides to build a tree house in the cool, green calm of
Central Park. Includes a note about the real Bob Redman.
Identifiers: LCCN 2017007608 | ISBN 9781454920717 (hc-plc)
Subjects: | CYAC: Tree houses--Fiction. | Central Park (New York,
N.Y.)--Fiction. | New York (N.Y.)--Fiction.
Classification: LCC PZ7.1.B674 Up 2018 | DDC [E]--dc23 LC record available at
https://lccn.loc.gov/2017007608

Distributed in Canada by Sterling Publishing Co., Inc.
c/o Canadian Manda Group, 664 Annette Street
Toronto, Ontario M6S 2C8, Canada
Distributed in the United Kingdom by GMC Distribution Services
Castle Place, 166 High Street, Lewes, East Sussex BN7 1XU, England
Distributed in Australia by NewSouth Books
45 Beach Street, Coogee NSW 2034, Australia

For information about custom editions, special sales, and premium and corporate purchases,
please contact Sterling Special Sales at 800-805-5489 or specialsales@sterlingpublishing.com.

Manufactured in China

Lot #:
2 4 6 8 10 9 7 5 3 1
12/17

sterlingpublishing.com
Design by Heather Kelly

UP IN THE LEAVES

The True Story of the Central Park Treehouses

By SHIRA BOSS

Illustrated by JAMEY CHRISTOPH

STERLING CHILDREN'S BOOKS
New York

Bob lived in the big city.
The city was very crowded.

It was crowded with buildings, stacked side by side.

It was crowded with strangers, packed onto trains.

It was crowded with trucks, honking their horns.

Bob didn't like all that rushing around, the eyes of so many people, all those feet on the ground.

He climbed up lampposts.

He snuck onto his building's roof.

He scaled the walls of the castle in the park.

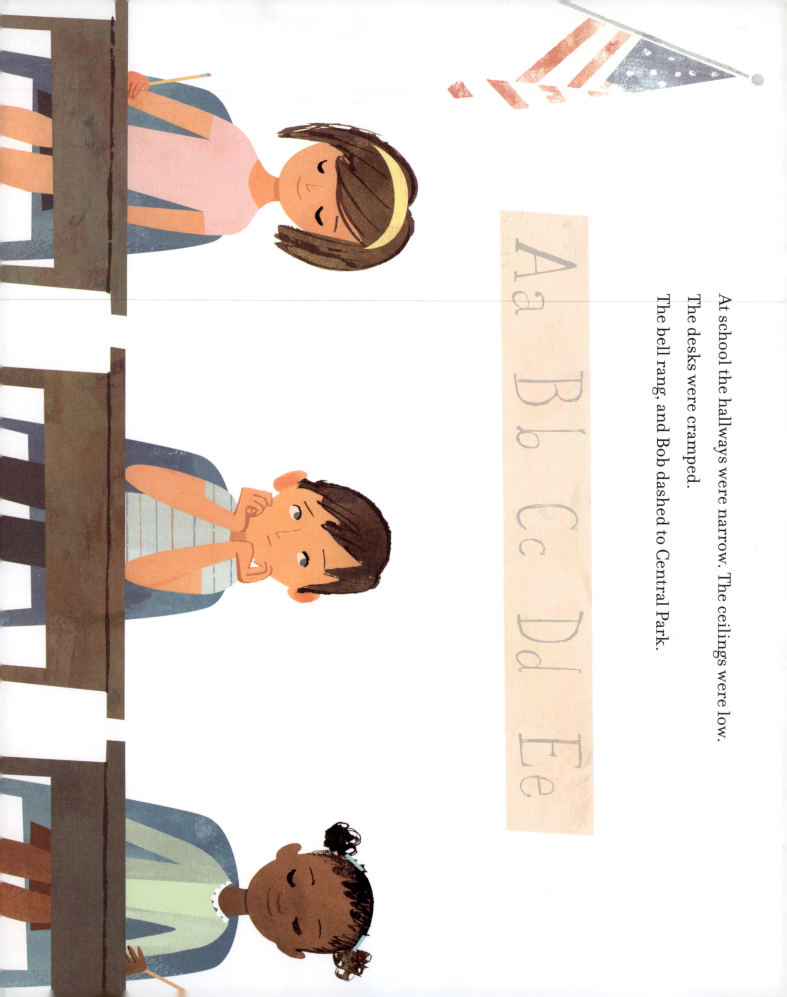

At school the hallways were narrow. The ceilings were low.

The desks were cramped.

The bell rang, and Bob dashed to Central Park.

The park was cool, green, calm.
People walked slowly or sat on the ground. Trees waved
their branches in the air, inviting him to come up.

He lifted himself onto a tree limb.
He pulled up to another and then
to the next. The bark made a path.
The leaves made a hideaway.

Up and down and up, he explored the trees: the fluffy, pink cherry tree . . . the sticky, pokey pine. . . .

He slipped through the door of a wide beech.

He stepped up the staircase of a tall oak.

Each tree was its own world, every limb an adventure.

He could see buildings and the people down below, so small.
But nobody could see him. This was his own secret spot.

He decided to stay.

Bob scavenged wood and rope from Dumpsters.
Tap, tap, tap, he hammered.
Whoosh, whoosh, whoosh, he sawed.
Loop, loop, loop, he knotted.

He read books in the hush and shared peanuts with the squirrels. He listened to the whirr of a dragonfly, the creaking of wood, the flapping of birds.

Every day after school, Bob's treehouse was waiting. He hugged the tree's trunk and scampered straight up. The city— *roar, clang, bang*—fell away.

One day, his treehouse was gone!
The squirrels had their nests. The birds had their roosts.
But the little boy no longer had a place of his own.

Bob started all over.

Tap, tap . . . .

Whoosh, whoosh . . . .

Loop, loop . . . .

His new treehouse was even bigger, and better hidden. When rain pelted down and wind bent the branches, Bob's treehouse rocked and swayed—he was a sailor on a ship at sea.

But fall came.
The leaves fell.
The treehouse was no
longer a secret.

Again it was taken away!
He no longer had a ship in the sky.

There was nothing to do except try again.

Up went a platform.

Up went the walls.

Up went the milk crates for tables and chairs.

He let down a rope . . . and up went some friends.

Bob stayed after sunset and mapped twinkling stars.

He even spotted planets. He became an astronaut, navigating the cosmos.

The seasons went on, and so did the treehouses. Each one was taken down—but Bob kept building.

Bob's mother worried.

"You'll be grown up soon. You can't stay up in trees!" She wanted him to go to work, like everyone else.

But that wasn't for him, shoulder-to-shoulder downtown: the traffic, the concrete, the air thick with smog.

Instead, he built the biggest treehouse of all.
Five levels and a bridge! Bob was very proud.

He loved drifting to sleep snuggled under the canopy of leaves.

One morning Bob woke up and heard voices far below.

"We know you're up there!" they yelled. "Come down!"

He sadly descended, like a fluttering leaf.
His adventure was over.
He was stuck on the ground.

But then, something lucky!

The man in charge of the park watched Bob come down.

He climbed like a squirrel, sure-footed and at ease.

"Come work in the park," the man said to Bob, "and take care of the trees."

A job in the trees?

"I would love to work here!" Bob said.

Every day, Bob walked to work in the park.
With his new ropes and saddle, he could climb any
tree, even the biggest.

He swung all over the branches, up and across,
from limb to limb. He snipped and he sawed and
he kept the trees healthy.

He stuck to his promise not to build any more
treehouses in the park.

But sometimes at night he slipped
out of bed and walked softly through
the city, back to his trees.

EPILOGUE

Bob Redman built twelve treehouses in New York City's Central Park, from the time he was thirteen until he was twenty-one. His friends helped him salvage building materials and construct the hideaways. He crafted each treehouse to have a special view: a balcony overlooking the tree canopy, or a leafy window framing the city skyline. He named them after stars. Studying the night sky was one of his favorite things to do in the magical treehouses.

Now Bob lives in an apartment near the park. Trees cover the roof, and it has skylights so he can gaze at the moon and stars. Still an arborist, Bob takes care of trees all over the city. He escapes high into the branches, just like when he built his treehouses.

"I went straight up," he says, "the higher the better—so only squirrels and birds could go higher."